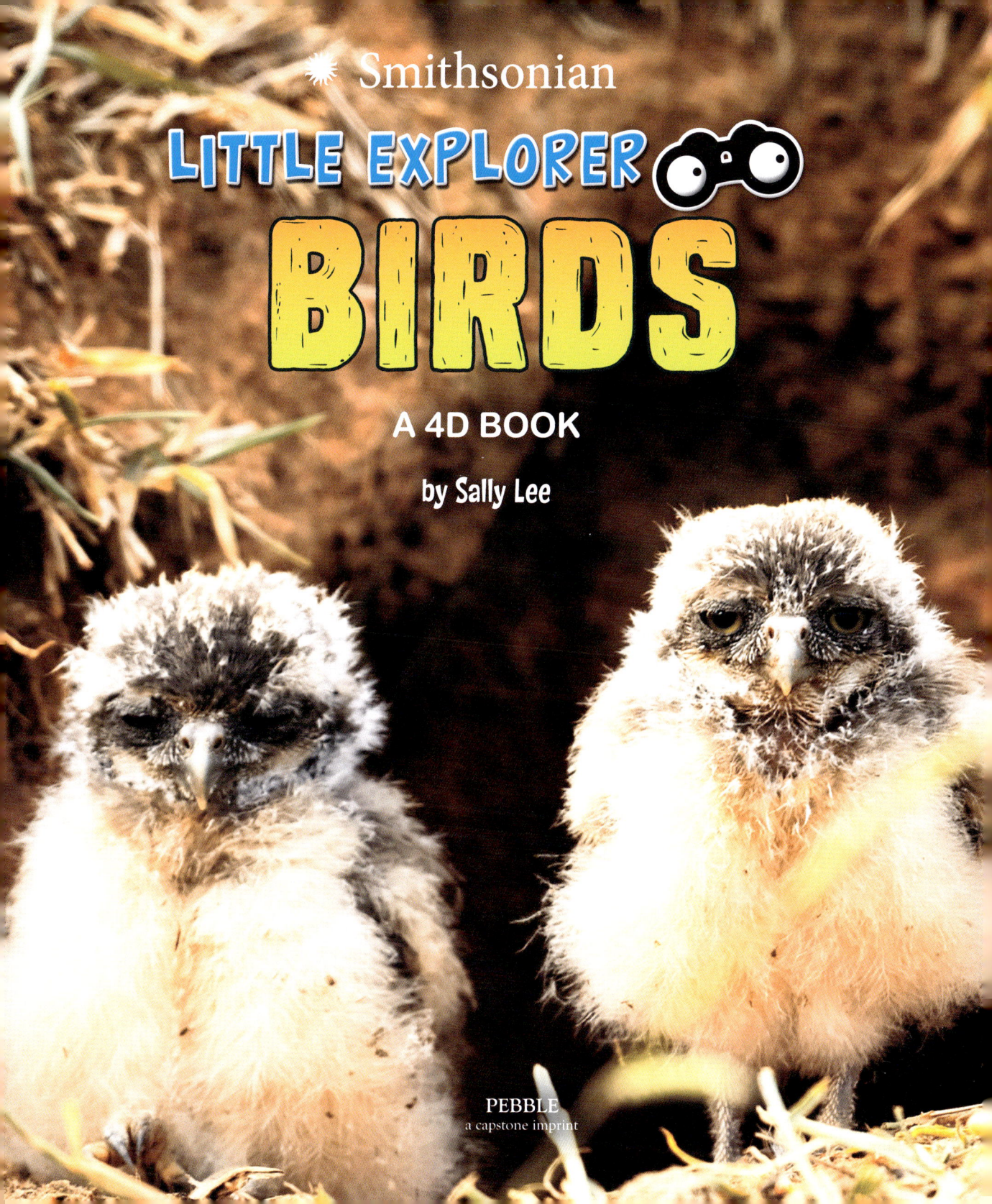

Smithsonian

LITTLE EXPLORER
BIRDS

A 4D BOOK

by Sally Lee

PEBBLE
a capstone imprint

Download the Capstone  app!

- Ask an adult to download the Capstone 4D app.
- Scan the cover and stars inside the book for additional content.

When you scan a spread, you'll find fun extra stuff to go with this book! You can also find these things on the web at www.capstone4D.com using the password: birds.26431

Smithsonian Little Explorer is published by Pebble, 1710 Roe Crest Drive, North Mankato, Minnesota 56003 www.mycapstone.com

Library of Congress Cataloging-in-Publication Data
Names: Lee, Sally, 1943– author.
Title: Birds : a 4D book / by Sally Lee.
Description: North Mankato, Minnesota : an imprint of Pebble, [2019] | Series: Smithsonian little explorer. Little zoologist | Audience: Age 4–8. | Includes bibliographical references and index. Identifiers: LCCN 2018004116 (print) | LCCN 2018008479 (ebook) | ISBN 9781543526554 (eBook PDF) | ISBN 9781543526431 (hardcover) | ISBN 9781543526493 (paperback) Subjects: LCSH: Birds—Juvenile literature. Classification: LCC QL676.2 (ebook) | LCC QL676.2 .L44 2019 (print) | DDC 598—dc23
LC record available at https://lccn.loc.gov/2018004116

Editorial Credits
Michelle Hasselius, editor; Kazuko Collins, designer; Svetlana Zhurkin, media researcher; Kris Wilfahrt, production specialist

Our very special thanks to Jen Zoon, communications specialist at Smithsonian's National Zoo, for her review. Capstone would also like to thank Kealy Gordon, Product Development Manager, and the following at Smithsonian Enterprises: Ellen Nanney, Licensing Manager; Brigid Ferraro, Vice President, Education and Consumer Products; and Carol LeBlanc, Senior Vice President, Education and Consumer Products.

Image Credits
Dreamstime: Fischer0182, cover, Michael Elliott, 6; Library of Congress, 4, 23 (top); Shutterstock: Ammit Jack, 18, Arto Hakola, 23 (bottom), Braam Collins, 21, David Watkins, 22, DejaVuDesigns, 28, Delmas Lehman, 5 (bottom), Don Blais, 8, Don Mammoser, 14 (right), Edwin Butter, 19, Eric Isselee, 2, Erni, 26, Gleb Ivanov, 20, Ian Dyball, 25, Ivan Godal, 12, John Carnemolla, 16, K Hanley CHDPhoto, 27, Kent Ellington, 29 (top), Lukas Gojda, 9 (top), Maria Jeffs, 15, mark smith nsb, 13, Marten_House, 24, Mauricio S Ferreira, 1, NatureDiver, 11, Neale Cousland, 17, Nick Biemans, 14 (left), Nick Fox, 9 (bottom), Paul Reeves Photography, 10, Richard Seeley, 29 (bottom); Smithsonian's National Zoo: Photo courtesy of Connor Mallon, 5 (top)

Design Elements by Shutterstock

Printed and bound in the United States.
PA021

TABLE OF CONTENTS

SMITHSONIAN'S NATIONAL ZOO

The Smithsonian's National Zoo got its start in 1887. During this time a Smithsonian scientist named William Temple Hornaday brought 15 North American animal species to Washington, D.C. Hornaday wanted to help endangered animals. The National Zoological Park officially opened in 1891. It grew into the 163-acre Smithsonian's National Zoo. Today curators, animal keepers, and scientists care for about 1,800 animals at the Zoo.

William Temple Hornaday

EXPERIENCE MIGRATION

By 2021 the Smithsonian's National Zoo will open Experience Migration, its latest exhibit. Visitors will learn about nearly 100 species of birds and the amazing trips they make each year. By studying their migration, scientists can learn about the threats faced by these birds.

The Smithsonian Conservation Biology Institute (SCBI) works with the Smithsonian's National Zoo to study endangered species and their habitats.

ABYSSINIAN GROUND HORNBILL

Abyssinian ground hornbills can be found in grasslands and savannas in north-central Africa. The birds are about 40 inches (102 cm) tall. They weigh 8 to 11 pounds (4 to 5 km).

Abyssinian ground hornbills have long feathers above their eyes. They look like eyelashes. The feathers protect their eyes from sand and dirt.

Abyssinian ground hornbills have large bills that they use to pick up small prey. The birds fling prey into the air, catch it, and then swallow it whole. Abyssinian ground hornbills eat small insects, small mammals, and reptiles such as snakes and lizards. There is one Abyssinian ground hornbill at the Zoo. He is named Karl. Keepers feed Karl mice, mealworms, and crickets.

Abyssinian ground hornbills would rather walk than fly. They travel up to 7 miles (11 kilometers) each day looking for food.

A NEW BILL FOR KARL

The Zoo's Abyssinian ground hornbill had a problem. Karl's lower bill was so worn down that he had trouble eating. The Zoo staff worked with the Smithsonian's National Museum of Natural History to make a new one. Using a 3D printer, Karl was able to get a replacement bill.

AMERICAN FLAMINGO

American flamingos are found in the Caribbean Sea and on the northern coast of South America. They live in shallow, salty water. These birds gather together in flocks.

Adult American flamingos are bright pink. This color comes from the food they eat. Flamingos stick their beaks upside-down in the water. Then they scoop up algae, fly larvae, shrimp, and mollusks. At the Zoo the keepers feed them flamingo pellets.

The American flamingo is one of the largest species of flamingos.

Flamingos build smooth, cone-shaped nests out of sticks, stones, and mud. Females usually lay one egg.

Flamingo chicks are white. They don't turn pink for several years.

Bald eagles are found in North America. At one time these birds were nearly extinct. By 1963 only 417 bald eagle pairs were left. Today they are no longer endangered.

Bald eagles have good eyesight. They can spot prey up to 1 mile (1.6 km) away. The birds grab fish or small mammals with their sharp talons. At the Zoo the bald eagles are fed rats, fish, chicken legs, and quail.

Bald eagles use the same nests year after year. The largest bald eagle nest ever found was 9.5 feet (2.9 m) wide. It was more than 19.7 feet (6 m) deep.

Bald eagles weigh from 6.5 to 14 pounds (3 to 6.5 kg).

Bald eagles can fly higher than 10,000 feet (3,048 m) in the air.

BROWN PELICAN

Brown pelicans live close to the shore along the coast of North, South, and Central America. The birds are 3 to 5 feet (0.9 to 1.5 m) long. They weigh more than 7 pounds (3 kg).

The brown pelican has a large pouch under its bill. The pouch can hold about 1 gallon (3.8 liters) of water.

When searching for food, brown pelicans fly over the ocean. Then they dive head first into the water. Brown pelicans come up with a pouch full of water and fish. The pelicans let the water drain out before swallowing their prey. At the Zoo the keepers feed the brown pelicans fish.

Brown pelicans have air sacs beneath their skin. These sacs help cushion the blow when the birds hit the water.

Brown pelicans were once threatened by the pesticide DDT. They are one of the first species to recover from the effects of DDT.

BURROWING OWL

Burrowing owls live mostly in open grasslands in western North America. They get their name from their underground nests. Instead of digging their own nests, burrowing owls move into empty burrows dug by ground squirrels and prairie dogs.

Burrowing owls can't move their eyes. They turn their heads around or tilt to the side to get a better look.

Burrowing owls line their nests with dung. This attracts insects for the owls to eat. Burrowing owls also eat rodents and frogs.

Burrowing owls are some of the smallest owls in North America. They grow to about 10 inches (25 cm) tall. They weigh a little more than 5 ounces (150 grams).

Emus are large, flightless birds. They are 4.9 to 6.2 feet (1.5 to 1.9 m) tall. Emus weigh between 66 and 100 pounds (30 and 45 kg). Female emus weigh more than males. Emus live only in Australia. They make their homes in grasslands, eucalyptus forests, and desert shrub lands.

Emus eat grass, seeds, fruits, flowers, and insects. They swallow large pebbles to help them grind up the food. At the Zoo emus are fed emu pellets and leafy vegetables.

Emus can't fly. But they can run up to 30 miles (48 km) per hour.

Emus are the second largest birds in the world.

KING VULTURE

King vultures live in forested tropical lowlands from Mexico to Argentina. They are 27 to 32 inches (69 to 81 cm) long. They weigh about 8 pounds (3.6 kg).

King vultures do not have feathers on their heads or necks. They don't have eyelashes.

King vultures eat rotting, dead animals called carrion. The birds use their sharp eyesight and sense of smell to find carrion. Then they rip it apart with their sharp claws and beaks. King vultures are fed rats and other meat at the Zoo.

King vultures have colorful heads and necks. They are orange, green, yellow, and purplish blue.

KORI BUSTARD

Kori bustards live in grasslands and lightly wooded areas in eastern and southern Africa. Kori bustards are the heaviest flying birds in the world. But they rarely leave the ground. They weigh up to 42 pounds (19 kg) and stand nearly 4 feet (1.2 m) tall.

Kori bustards grab insects and small invertebrates off the ground. They also eat small mammals, lizards, snakes, seeds, and wild melons. At the Zoo the keepers feed them mice and insects.

Male kori bustards attract females by puffing out the feathers on their necks.

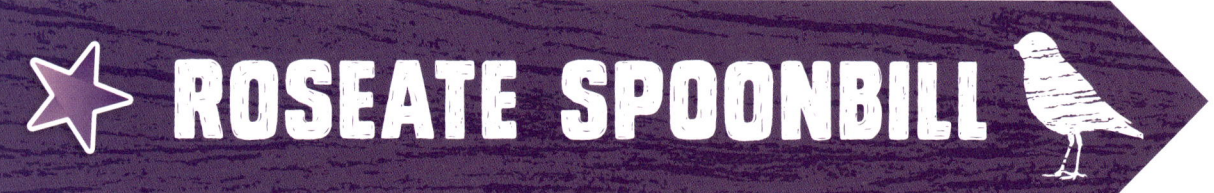

ROSEATE SPOONBILL

Roseate spoonbills live in shallow water throughout the southern United States and South America. The birds are about 2.5 feet (80 cm) tall. They weigh from 2.5 to 4 pounds (1.2 to 1.8 kg).

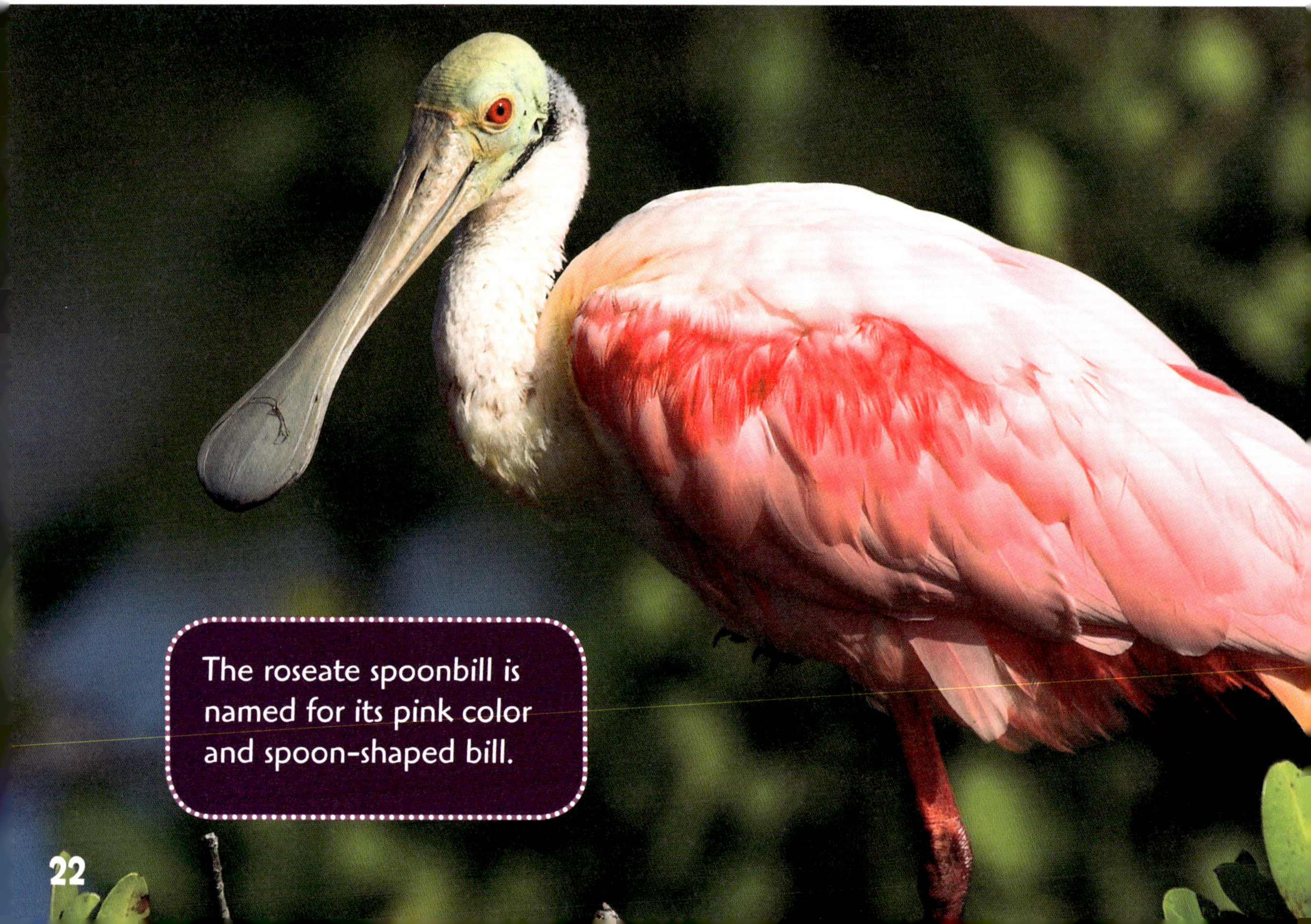

The roseate spoonbill is named for its pink color and spoon-shaped bill.

Roseate spoonbills move their bills back and forth in the water to find food. They eat minnows, small crustaceans, insects, and plants. Scientists think these birds get their pink coloring from the crustaceans they eat. At the Zoo they are fed flamingo pellets, sea duck pellets, and insects.

Roseate spoonbills nearly went extinct in the early 1900s. They were hunted for their feathers, which were used to make women's hats and fans.

RÜPPELL'S GRIFFON VULTURE

Rüppell's griffon vultures are found in Africa. They are critically endangered. This means these birds have the greatest risk of becoming extinct. Deadly pesticides, hunting, loss of food, and loss of habitat are decreasing their population.

At the Zoo, Rüppell's griffon vultures are fed pellets, bones, rats, and rabbits.

Rüppell's griffon vultures are the world's highest-flying birds. In 1973 one of these birds was sucked into the engine of an airplane that was flying 37,000 feet (11,278 m) in the air. That's higher than Mount Everest, the world's tallest mountain.

VULTURE LESSONS

Keepers train animals to participate in their daily care. The Zoo has two Rüppell's griffon vultures—Natalie and Tuck. The pair needed to learn how to go inside when called. Keepers put bits of meat on the end of a training target. They used this target to teach Natalie and Tuck to go inside.

SUNBITTERN

Sunbitterns live in tropical habitats in Guatemala and northern Brazil. They are about 18 inches (45.7 cm) long. Sunbitterns look like brown birds. But when they spread their wings, they reveal large orange and brown spots.

Sunbitterns use their long necks and sharp bills to stab fish, amphibians, crustaceans, and insects. At the Zoo the keepers feed them pellets, mice, mealworms, corn grubs, and crickets.

Sunbitterns can fly, but usually walk slowly on their thin orange legs.

If a predator threatens a sunbittern's chick, one parent will pretend to have a broken wing. This distracts the predator. Then the other parent can get the chick to safety.

The oldest sunbittern at the Smithsonian's National Zoo lived to age 33. It was in the Amazonia exhibit.

WHOOPING CRANE

Whooping cranes are North America's tallest birds. They stand 5 feet (1.5 m) tall. These cranes almost became extinct when early settlers hunted them and destroyed their habitats. Today there are about 300 whooping cranes. These birds are still endangered.

Whooping cranes only weigh about 15 pounds (7 kg). This is because their bones are hollow.

Whooping cranes got their name from their loud calls.

Whooping cranes live in prairie wetlands, ponds, and marshes. They eat blue crabs, small fish, reptiles, insects, and plants. At the Zoo they are fed crane pellets, insects, and small fish.

GLOSSARY

algae—small plants without roots or stems that grow in water

amphibian—a cold-blooded animal with a backbone; amphibians live in water when young and can live on land as adults

bill—the hard front part of a bird's mouth

burrow—a tunnel or hole in the ground made or used by an animal

crustacean—a sea animal with an outer skeleton

curator—a person in charge of an exhibit

endangered—at risk of dying out

extinct—no longer living

flock—a group of the same kind of animal; members of flocks live, travel, and eat together

grassland—a large, open area where grass and low plants grow

habitat—the natural place and conditions in which an animal lives

hollow—empty on the inside

mammal—a warm-blooded animal that breathes air and has hair or fur; females feed milk to their young

marsh—an area of wet, low land covered in grasses and low plants

migration—the regular movement of animals as they search different places for food

mollusk—a soft-bodied creature that usually has a shell

pellet—a small, hard piece of food

pesticide—a poisonous chemical used to kill insects and fungi

prey—an animal hunted by another animal for food

savanna—a flat, grassy area of land with few or no trees

shallow—an area of water that is not very deep

species—a group of plants or animals that have the same ancestor and share common characteristics

talon—a long, sharp claw

CRITICAL THINKING QUESTIONS

1. Bald eagles have talons. What are talons? How do bald eagles use them?

2. Describe how brown pelicans catch their prey.

3. How do sunbitterns protect their chicks from predators?

READ MORE

Hill, Melissa. *Burrowing Owls*. Owls. North Mankato, Minn.: Capstone Press, 2016.

Kissock, Heather. *Bald Eagles*. Little Backyard Animals. New York: AV2 by Weigl, 2017.

Omoth, Tyler. *Bald Eagles*. Animals of North America. Mankato, Minn.: Focus Readers, 2017.

INTERNET SITES

Use FactHound to find Internet sites related to this book.

Visit www.facthound.com

Just type in 9781543526431 and go.

Super-cool stuff! Check out projects, games and lots more at **www.capstonekids.com**

INDEX